SOMETHING NEW TO DO

Written by Ski Michaels
Illustrated by Jan Palmer

Troll Associates

Library of Congress Cataloging in Publication Data

⎯

Something new to do.

Summary: Constantly in search of new things to do,
a young octopus has some scary experiences.
    [1. Octopus—Fiction. 2. Marine animals—Fiction]
I. Palmer, Jan, ill.   II. Title.
PZ7.P3656SO   1986   [E]   85-14021
ISBN 0-8167-0634-4 (lib. bdg.)
ISBN 0-8167-0635-2 (pbk.)

SOMETHING NEW TO DO

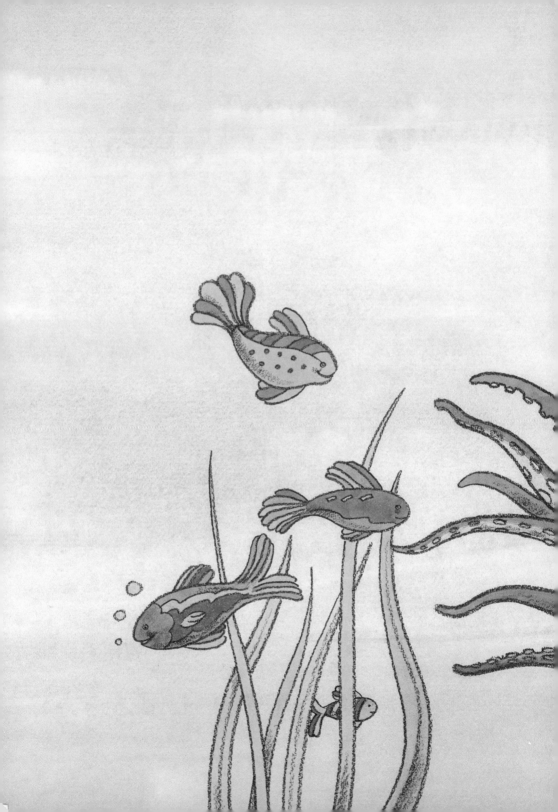

Elroy was special. He had eight
long, wiggly arms. His arms had
a special name. They were called
"tentacles." Elroy was an octopus.

The ocean was Elroy's home.
There were lots of things to do in
the ocean. It was a fun place to
live.

He went swimming. Swimming
was fun.

He went fishing. Fishing was fun.

Often he sat on a big, black rock and juggled shells. Juggling was fun. But sometimes while juggling, his tentacles got all tangled up. His arms ended up in knots. What a mess!

It took hours to untangle his
arms and untie the knots. Poor,
poor Elroy.

One day Elroy said, "I'm tired of
swimming. I'm tired of fishing.
I'm tired of juggling. I need
something new to do."
Off he went to do something
new.

After awhile he saw something
new. It was buried in the sand.
"What is that?" Elroy asked.

"To find out I must dig," he
said. "Digging in the sand is
something new to do."
So dig he did.

Elroy dug up the new thing. But
the new thing did not want to be
dug up. It wanted to stay buried
in the sand.

The thing was a hermit crab. It wanted to be left alone. A hermit crab is not very friendly.

"This is fun," said Elroy.
"This is not fun," cried the
hermit crab.
The hermit crab pinched Elroy.

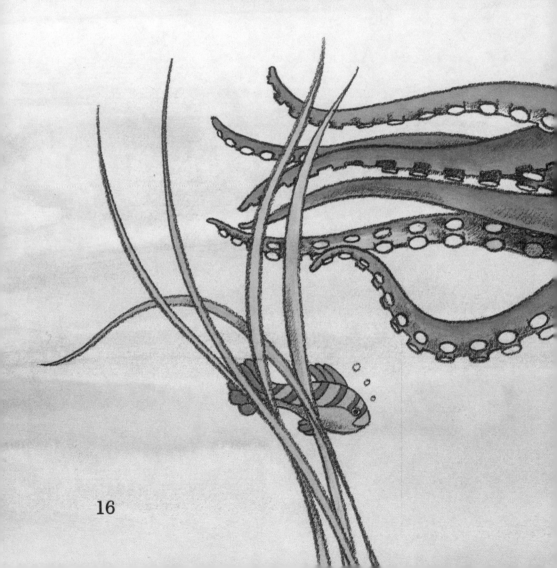

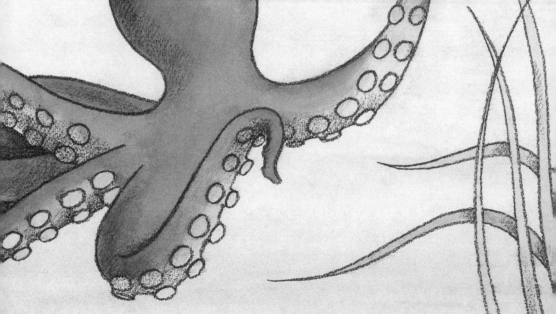

"Ouch," cried Elroy. "Getting pinched is not fun at all!"

Elroy left the hermit crab alone.
"I want something new to do
that does not pinch," said Elroy.
So away he went.

Elroy swam this way. Nothing
new there. Elroy swam that
way. Nothing new there.

He swam every which way.
It was not easy to find something
new to do.

"There is something," cried
Elroy, "something new. It is big.
It is dark. I think it is the big,
dark mouth of a cave. I like
caves!"

Elroy swam in. He swam into
the mouth of the big, dark cave.

"This cave looks funny," said
Elroy. "It has teeth. It has a big
tongue. *Yipes!* This is not a cave!
It is the mouth of a whale."

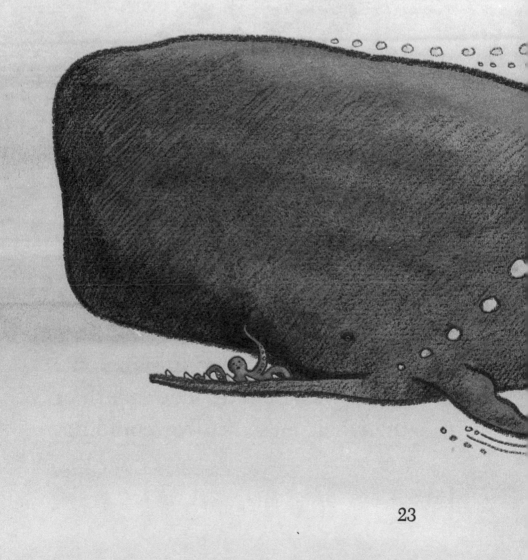

Quickly, Elroy tried to swim out.
But it was too late. The mouth of
the whale closed. Elroy could not
get out.

"Help! Help! Help!" Elroy
yelled.
His yells made bubbles. The
bubbles tickled the whale's
tongue.

Help! Help! Help!

"Ah-choo!" sneezed the whale.
Out came Elroy. Out he came
very fast! The sneeze sent him
spinning top over tentacles.
Around and around he went.

AH-CHOO

BONK! Elroy crashed into
something. It was the mast pole
of an old sunken ship.

Elroy grabbed onto the mast. He wrapped his tentacles around it. ZIP! Down the mast pole he slid.

THUD! He landed on the deck!
OUCH! He landed so hard his
backside hurt.

There on the deck Elroy sat.
He was sore and dizzy. He had
nothing new to do. Poor Elroy.

Finally his head stopped
spinning. He looked around.
"This is an old pirate ship!" he
yelled. "Exploring a sunken ship
is something new to do."

Elroy began to explore. The
pirate ship was spooky. It was
scary. It made Elroy shake.

In an old room, Elroy found something special. It was a pirate chest. He opened the lid.

"Oh boy! A sunken treasure,"
cried Elroy. "Playing with pirate
treasure is something new to do."

34

Elroy sat on the chest. He put a
crown on his head. He put rings
on his eight arms.
"I wonder how I look?" he asked.

A spooky voice answered.
"You look good enough to eat,"
the voice said.

"Who is that?" Elroy asked.
He looked around. He saw a
scary shark. The shark wanted to
eat Elroy.

Elroy began to shake. Off fell the
crown. Off fell the rings.

"Goodbye," said Elroy.
He squirted black octopus ink in
the shark's eye. That was a
special trick of his. The shark
could not see Elroy.

Quickly, he swam up, up, and
away from the sunken ship.
"I want something new to do
that is not so scary," said Elroy.

Elroy sat on a big rock. What
new thing could he do now?
He wanted something that did
not pinch. He wanted something
that did not make him dizzy.
He wanted something that was
not scary.

"I want something new to do,"
he cried. "But what?"

"You can play with me," said
someone new. "My name is Edna.
I live here."
Edna was special. She had eight
long, wiggly arms, just like Elroy.
Edna was an octopus, too.

Elroy smiled at Edna.
"My name is Elroy," he said.
Edna smiled back at Elroy.

Elroy said, "Playing with a
friend is something new to do.
What can we do, friend?"

Edna answered, "We can go
swimming. We can go fishing.
We can go juggle clam shells."